This book belongs to

SIMON AND SCHUSTER
This book first published in Great Britain in 2014
by Simon and Schuster UK Ltd,
1st Floor, 222 Gray's Inn Road, London WC1X 8HB
A CBS Company
Shimmer the Magic Ice Pony first published in 2011
Silver the Magic Snow Pony first published in 2009
Text copyright © 2009, 2011, 2014 Sarah KilBride
llustrations copyright © 2009, 2011, 2014 Sophie Tilley
Concept © 2009 Simon and Schuster UK
A CIP catalogue record for this book is available from
the British Library upon request
ISBN HB: 978 1 4711 2357 3
ISBN PB: 978 1 4711 2291 0
Printed in China
10 9 8 7 6 5 4 3 2 1

Princess Evie's Ponies

The Magical Winter Ponies

Sarah KilBride

Illustrated by Sophie Tilley

SIMON AND SCHUSTER

London   New York   Sydney   Toronto   New Delhi

Princess Evie's Ponies

Shimmer the Magic Ice Pony

Sarah KilBride

Illustrated by Sophie Tilley

It was such a cold day at Starlight Stables that even the water buckets had frozen! Princess Evie gave each of her ponies fresh water and straw.

"Now, who would like to warm up with an adventure?" she said. You see, Princess Evie's ponies were magic ponies. Whenever Evie rode them, she was whisked away on a magical adventure in a faraway land.

"Shimmer!" said Evie. "Would you like to come?"

Shimmer tossed her long silver mane. She loved adventures!

When Sparkles the kitten heard Evie getting her rucksack

of useful things, he raced across the yard to join them.

Off they cantered, through the
frosty fields to the tunnel of trees.
Evie closed her eyes. Where would the
tunnel take them today?

Shimmer's hooves echoed as they walked out of a huge ice cave.

Princess Evie was lovely and snug in the snow boots and furry coat that she now wore. Ice crystals glinted in Shimmer's mane and tail, and rows of tiny icicles twinkled from her reins. Outside the cave, sat a little ice pixie holding onto a big bag.

"Hello, I'm Freya," said the pixie. "I've been waiting for you. I knew your magic ice pony would bring you here."

Freya handed Evie an invitation.

"It's for the Ice Queen's birthday party," she said.

"How exciting!" Evie gasped. "But I haven't got a present for her."

"We can give her this," said Freya, and she pulled
a beautiful rainbow balloon from her bag.

Just then, an icy gust of wind blew the
balloon out of Freya's hands. Sparkles
leapt up and caught its ribbons
but the wind was so strong that the
balloon lifted him up into the air.

"Hold on, Sparkles!" shouted Princess Evie.
Evie and Freya jumped onto Shimmer's back.

Shimmer galloped through the trees,
and jumped across mountain streams,
following Sparkles as he rose higher and higher.

"Miaow!" yelped Sparkles, still clinging
to the balloon's silk ribbons.

"Don't worry," said Evie, "we'll get you down!"

Princess Evie searched through her rucksack
of useful things and found a ball, a notebook
and a shiny red whistle.

"Oh dear!" sighed Evie. "None of these things can help."

"I have an idea," Freya smiled. "Watch!"

Freya began to play a strange tune
on the whistle. Instantly, two
glittering snowflakes fell from
the clouds and, as they fluttered
down, they turned into . . .

. . . snowflake fairies!

The fairies flew up to Sparkles
and caught him in their arms.

Shimmer neighed, and Evie and Freya cheered
as the snowflake fairies gently floated down,
bringing Sparkles with them.

Sparkles felt a little dizzy but he wasn't hurt.
"You're so brave," said Evie. She gave him
a big hug.

"Thank you, snowflake fairies."

Suddenly, there was a huge
BANG! The rainbow balloon
caught on a sharp branch and burst.

"Oh dear! What can we give the Queen now?" asked Evie.

"We can make a tiara and necklace," said Freya. "Look!"
The balloon's silk ribbons were covered in icicles and
snowflakes. They glittered like diamonds.

Everyone set to work, making the Queen's beautiful birthday presents.

Soon the icicle tiara and snowflake necklace shimmered.

It was time for the party!

Off Shimmer trotted, taking Evie, Freya and Sparkles to

the Ice Palace. The snowflake fairies followed above.

The Ice Palace glittered and sparkled. All the ice pixies were there to celebrate. Even the penguins had come, dressed in their smartest suits to perform their favourite songs.

The Ice Queen looked beautiful in her tiara and matching necklace.
"Would you like to help me blow out my candles?" the Queen
asked Evie. "There are so many of them!"

Soon the moon shone in the sky. Princess Evie yawned.
She knew that Shimmer and Sparkles must be tired too.
It was time to go home.

"Thank you so much for inviting us," she said to the
Ice Queen. "And thank you, Freya."
"Come again soon!" smiled Freya, as she gave them all a big hug.

Princess Evie waved to her
new friend as she disappeared
through the tunnel of trees.

When they got back to Starlight Stables, large snowflakes began to fall.
"It's snowing!" said Evie. As she put a warm blanket over Shimmer,
she noticed a glittery silk ribbon in her mane.

"A snowflake necklace!" said Evie. "Thank you, Freya.
And thank you, Shimmer, for helping Sparkles.
What a very brave ice pony you are!"

"Miaow!" agreed Sparkles.

Princess Evie's Ponies

Silver the Magic Snow Pony

Sarah KilBride

Illustrated by Sophie Tilley

What a busy morning at Starlight Stables! Princess Evie had been busy mucking out her ponies' stalls with the help of her kitten Sparkles. "That was hard work!" sighed Evie. "Now it's time for an adventure. Who's coming today?"

You see, Evie's ponies weren't just any old ponies. They were magic ponies! Whenever Evie rode them, she was whisked away on a magical adventure in a faraway land.

Silver neighed and shook her long mane.

"OK, Silver," smiled Evie. "It's you!" Silver was a small pony

with a soft white coat like fallen snow.

"Come on, Sparkles!" called Evie. But Sparkles wouldn't jump up.

"What's wrong?" she asked. Then Evie realised.

She had forgotten her rucksack full of useful things!

Quickly, she scooped up the rucksack and Sparkles.

Silver cantered towards the
tunnel of trees. Evie closed her eyes.
Where would the tunnel take them today?

Princess Evie gasped as she opened her eyes to a wonderful snow covered world. Now she was wearing a fluffy pink cloak, woolly mittens and snug boots.

Silver's mane and tail sparkled with icicles, and swirling patterns of frost glittered on her bridle and saddle.

As they plodded through the snow, they met two little snow fairies pulling a VERY big sleigh!

"Where are you going with such a big sleigh?" asked Evie.
"We're going ice-skating on Lake Perla," said the snow fairies.
"Do you want to come?"

"Oooh, yes please," replied Evie, excitedly.
"I love skating. My pony, Silver,
is really strong. She can pull your
sleigh if you like."

Soon they were all gliding towards Lake Perla.

Snuggled up in the back of the sleigh, Evie and the
snow fairies sang jolly songs as snowflakes floated
down and landed on their noses.

Suddenly, without warning, Silver stopped.

"What is it, Silver?" asked Evie.

"Look!" cried the snow fairies, pointing. There, at the bottom of a huge snowdrift, was a tiny polar bear cub. He looked at them with big sad eyes.

"I've lost my mummy and daddy," he quivered.

"Please help me!"

The snow fairies knew that the polar bears lived in the North and Evie knew that, with Silver pulling the sleigh, they could get the little cub home before dark and still get to Lake Perla in time for skating. There was just one problem — which way was north?

Sparkles had an idea!

He padded over to the rucksack full of useful things

and found a shoelace, a pencil and a compass.

"Well done, Sparkles," cheered Evie.

They all watched the hand of the compass spin

and then point northwards. Off they sped.

As the snow got thicker and thicker, Evie and the snow fairies pulled up their warm hoods. Sparkles and the little polar bear cub huddled up. But soon the snow was flying all around them and Silver couldn't see through it.

They were lost in a blizzard!

"I want my mummy!" sobbed the little cub.

"Don't worry," said Evie. "We'll find her somehow."

But even Evie was feeling a little scared, stuck in the snow.

Just then, there was a loud roaring noise.

"HELP!" cried Evie and the snow fairies together.

But there was no need to worry.

"Momma!" squealed the bear cub and he leapt out of the sleigh, right into the arms of his mummy. "We've been searching for you everywhere," said Mummy Bear and she gave her baby a big hug.

"Thank you for rescuing our little baby," said Daddy Bear. "How can we ever repay you?"

"Well," said Evie. "Perhaps you could tell us how to get to Lake Perla?"

"We can do better than that," smiled Daddy Bear.

"Come on, bears. All together!"

The bears helped pull the sleigh out of the blizzard.

Then they gathered around and began humming. The sound echoed through the air and their icy breath spiralled up to the sky. Princess Evie looked up to see a swirl of snowflakes above the sleigh.

The flakes whirled and whizzed around them. As they whirled faster and faster, they lifted Silver and the sleigh up into the air. "We're flying!" cried Evie and the snow fairies as they climbed higher and higher into the air. "Bye-bye, bears and thank you!"

They flew over deep snowdrifts and herds of reindeer scraping at the snow. They looked down and saw snow foxes playing together.

Before they could catch their breath, the sleigh landed gently on the banks of Lake Perla. "That was amazing!" gasped Princess Evie. Everyone cheered when the sleigh arrived and soon the frozen lake was full of snow fairies practising their ice dances.

"Come on, Evie!" giggled the snow fairies. Evie put on her ice skates and glided onto the ice. Music floated softly across the frozen lake and all the fairies clapped and sang.

After their dances, Princess Evie and the snow fairies warmed
up with delicious cups of hot chocolate.

Then it was time for Evie, Sparkles and Silver to go home.
Princess Evie gave the snow fairies big hugs.
"Thank you for a wonderful adventure," she said.
"Don't forget to come back soon," smiled the snow fairies.

Off Silver cantered, back through
the snow to the tunnel of trees. Evie turned
and waved to the two little snow fairies.

Back at Starlight Stables, Princess Evie brushed out Silver's mane. Something fell and landed on the ground with a tinkle.

It was a little jewelled purse. Inside, there
were two little snowflake hair clips.

"Thank you, snow fairies," smiled Princess Evie.
"And thank you, Silver. You're a VERY
special snow pony!"
"Miaow!" agreed Sparkles.

Collect all the Princess Evie books

Neptune the M...

Star the Ma...

Silver the Magic...no...

Sprinkles the Ma... Cupcake Pon...

Shimmer the ...agic Ice Pony

Indigo the Magic R...nb...w ony

Willow the M...

Diamond...

Confetti the Magic ...